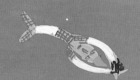

# さよなら、
# ミセス
# カックルマン

マイラ カルマン

# SAYONARA, MRS. KACKLEMAN

BY MAIRA KALMAN

# PUFFIN BOOKS

PUBLISHED BY THE PENGUIN GROUP
VIKING PENGUIN
A DIVISION OF PENGUIN BOOKS USA INC
375 HUDSON ST. NEW YORK NY 10014 USA
PENGUIN BOOKS LTD.
27 WRIGHTS LANE, LONDON W8 5TZ ENGLAND
PENGUIN BOOKS, AUSTRALIA LTD.:
RINGWOOD, VICTORIA, AUSTRALIA
PENGUIN BOOKS CANADA LTD
2801 JOHN STREET
MARKHAM, ONTARIO, CANADA L3R 1B4
PENGUIN BOOKS (N.Z.) LTD,
182-190 WAIRAU ROAD
AUCKLAND 10, NEW ZEALAND
PENGUIN BOOKS LTD, REGISTERED OFFICES
HARMONDSWORTH, MIDDLESEX, ENGLAND
FIRST PUBLISHED IN THE UNITED STATES
OF AMERICA BY VIKING PENGUIN
A DIVISION OF PENGUIN USA INC 1989
PUBLISHED IN PICTURE PUFFINS 1991
1 3 5 7 9 10 8 6 4 2

LIBRARY OF CONGRESS CATALOG
CARD NUMBER: 91-52915
ISBN 0-14-054159-4
PRINTED IN JAPAN

MY THANKS
TO THE REAL
HIROKO
FOR BRINGING
ME TO THE
REAL JAPAN
AND TO THE
REAL
KACKLEMAN
FAMILY,
TUTTI

DESIGN BY M + Co. N.Y.C.

THIS TOUPÉE IS KILLING ME.

# SAYONARA, MRS. KACKLEMAN

BY
MAIRA KALMAN

Puffin Books

THIS SKIRT IS FROM FRANCE.

"Lulu, I want to go there."
My little brother Alexander
whispered that to me
while we were watching
a funny opera called
*The Mikado.*
"Where?" I asked.
"To that place where they
are singing. Pajan."
"Not Pajan, it's Japan."
"Yes, that's where I want
to go. Now. Please."

I had a piano lesson the next day with the dreaded Mrs. Kackleman, so it seemed like a great idea. "Yes," I smiled, "I will take you."

I called the travel agent, Mr. Google.

"Hello, Mr. Google. Two seats on the Japan plane please. Thank you Mr. Google." We kissed our parents good-bye. They said come back soon. Bring back presents.

And off we went.
Into the blue sky. To Japan.
Which as I explained
to the miniature midget
(as I sometimes call my brother)
is a skinny island next to China
and the people are Japanese.
"Japansneeze!? They always sneeze?"
"No," I yelled. "Not sneeze, *nese*."
"Knees? They walk on their knees?"
he screeched.
"No," I screamed. "They are
of Japan, Japanese."
"Oh, I knew that," he said quietly.

We landed in a
city called Tokyo.
The people are very polite
and are always saying,
"*Domo arigato gozaimasu,*"
which means,
"Thank you very very much."
The alphabet looks like
little stick pictures.
We looked at a sign.
Alexander thought it meant
DON'T JUMP ON THE BED
but I knew it meant
TWO HEADS
ARE BETTER THAN ONE

We hopped into a red taxi with a driver in white gloves and sharp black hair. Everyone in Japan has black hair. Not red, not yellow, not green, just black. Narrow streets whizzed by. Little houses and stores. People on bicycles, people walking.

Our hotel was a *ryokan*, which is like a Japanese home. You take your shoes off before you step inside, so you must make sure that your socks don't have holes. You walk on mats called *tatami*. And you sleep on the floor on a cushy pad called a futon and cover yourself with a quilt as soft as a cloud. We sat on the floor at a table and had jasmine tea and rice crackers.

Outside our window
we heard music.
Under fluttering
cherry blossoms
women danced to the
playing of flutes.

The door knocked.
In walked our guide,
Hiroko. She
was going to show
us many places.
Alexander made up
a poem that I was
very proud of.

Hey Hiroko,
are you loco?
Would you like
a cup of cocoa?

We opened the present that Hiroko brought— a book with pictures of schoolchildren many years ago. They were dressed in beautiful robes called kimonos. Now children wear school uniforms and the girls have braids that point to the ground. We wanted to meet the children at school. We jumped up. "I will take you," said Hiroko. We went to the subway.

The subway was shining and quiet. The workers stood in crisp uniforms. The train smoothed into the station and was full of people. We were like marshmallows all stuffed together in a bag bouncing along, but nobody stuck their elbow in my ear.

In the school, the children bowed hello, singing a good morning song. Other children were reading a story about a man who traveled to a magic castle under the sea on the back of a turtle. Other children were learning music and the birds chirped on trees.

Walking in the sun,
we passed a man
sitting on a bench.
His black, crooked cane
poked the ground
and looked like a snake.

We went to a noodle
restaurant. Alexander
said they served
oodles and poodles
of noodles.
The waiter brought
us little hot wet
white towels. We
wiped our hands.
The bowls of noodles
arrived with chopsticks.
Alexander's chopsticks
kept flipping and flying
through the air.
I taught him how to
use them and we
all slurped our noodles,
which is a perfectly
perfectly fine thing
to do in Japan.

Strolling along, we came
to a rock garden.
There were big rocks
that were like
islands. All around them,
sand was raked
into patterns like the
ocean. And even if one
tiny leaf fell on the sand,
a gardener would come
and pluck it away using
a long pole with a pin
on the end. In the pond,
big spotted carp wiggled
to our feet. The quiet
was so quiet that the
quiet filled the air.

We went to eat.
At the restaurant
we took off our shoes.
Alexander was sure
they were cooking
our shoes.
Shoe soup?
Shoe sandwiches?
Shoe pie?
But really it was
rice and vegetables tied
with tiny seaweed bows.

It was a dreamy night. We wandered through the city and went to a movie called *Godzilla*. This giant lizard clomped around Tokyo scaring everyone and Alexander said, "That Godzilla is my friend."

The next morning Hiroko came to our door. "This is a fishy morning," she announced. "I would like to take you to the fish market." There are little places to eat raw fish called sushi, which frog boy (as I sometimes call my slippery brother) calls squishy.

We walked to an old temple where people tied zillions of little pieces of paper with wishes on them to a tree. People pulled long heavy ropes that made big bells ring. And the sound of the ringing would ring up to the sky. Alexander wished for a flying bike and I wished for a dancing dog.

"And now," said Hiroko, "we will take a bath." "Now? Here?" "No, up there." She pointed to a mountain. We got on a little wooden train.

In the middle of a pine forest was the bath. Alexander wanted to jump right in, but there are things you must do first. Like take off all your clothes. We sat on benches, scrubbed like crazy and rinsed with buckets of water. Then we scrubbed some more and rinsed some more. Then we stepped into the steamy water, sat down, closed our eyes and the smell of pines filled our noses and made us smile.

Extremely clean, we went to a fancy café. Alexander wrote poems. I blinked at the chandeliers. Our waiter curved over us with small sweet mountains of green ice.

Hiroko said, "I want
to take you to
a play called Noh.
"Yes?" asked Alexander.
"No, not yes, Noh," I said.
"Oh no?"
"No, not no, *Noh.*"
"Oh, Noh," smiled
Alexander understanding.
"Well let's go!"
There were dragons and
people in masks and nobody
moved for one hour including
Alexander who fell asleep.

The next morning the door knocked and in walked Hiroko. She said, "Today I would like to take you on a very fast train. So fast it is called the Bullet Train." The train was so fast we were back before we left. That's fast.

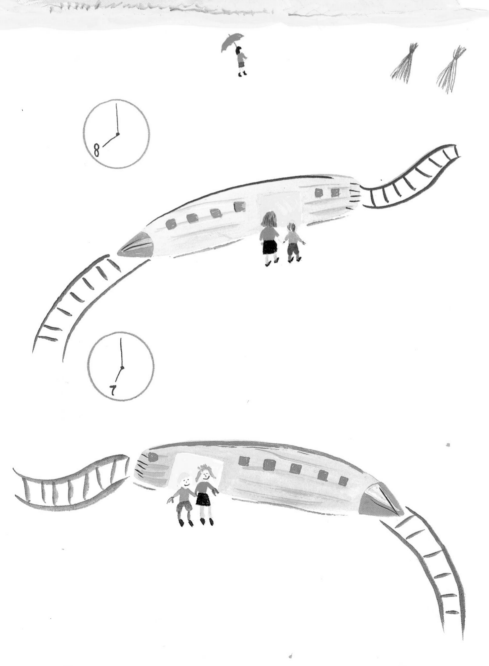

Hiroko's best friend, a beautiful movie star named Fujiko gave us a good-bye party. Paper lanterns swung in the breeze. The evening was warm. Alexander, my little brother spoke his farewell poem.

Oh, Japan kids
you eat raw fish
a crazy dish
the way you bow
is really wow
Hai is yes
and Noh is a show
I've got to iku
which means go.
Sayonara and good-bye
Please don't cry
You might swallow
a fly.

Full of presents we flew,
into the arms of our parents.
We were back. Back to the
twins Salomé and Mona.
Back to the little green man
who floats on the ceiling,
and back to our good
friend Bruno and
his invisible paintings.
But that is another story.

CHADO